This book belongs to

To my husband's children, Karimi, Ciku, Mwangi & Wajii, all my love.
Wanuri

To my supportive and loving sister, Sara.
Manuela

American edition published in 2017 by Lantana Publishing Ltd.
www.lantanapublishing.com

First published in the United Kingdom in 2017 by
Lantana Publishing Ltd., London.
info@lantanapublishing.com

Text © Wanuri Kahiu 2017
Illustration © Manuela Adreani 2017

The moral rights of the author and illustrator have been asserted.

Distributed in the United States and Canada by Lerner Publishing Group, Inc.
241 First Avenue North
Minneapolis, MN 55401 USA

For reading levels and more information, look for this title at
www.lernerbooks.com.

Printed and bound in Hong Kong.
Cataloguing-in-Publication Data Available.

ISBN-13: 978-1-911373-12-4
eBook ISBN: 978-1-911373-21-6

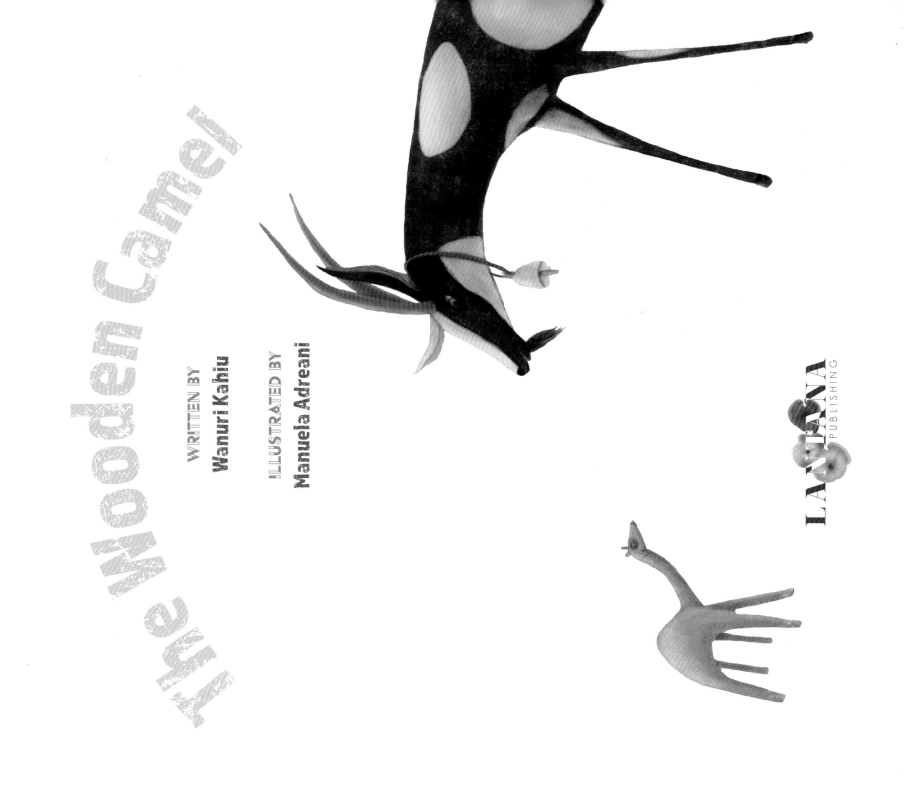

The Wooden Camel

WRITTEN BY
Wanuri Kahiu

ILLUSTRATED BY
Manuela Adreani

LANTANA
PUBLISHING

Etabo dreams about racing camels.

He thinks it will feel like flying.

He knows he will surely beat his older

brother Lopeyok when they race.

All his brothers and sisters make fun of Etabo. He's too small to race camels.

But Etabo doesn't care. He knows he will be the best camel racer ever.

One day, their father tells them they have to sell all the camels for money to buy water.

Etabo is upset and wonders if he will ever have the chance to race.

When Etabo asks Akuj the
Sky God for help, Akuj says:
"Your dreams are enough."

With no camels to tend, Etabo and his sister Akiru and brother Lopeyok are sent to look after the goats.

It is a boring chore but Keti, their favorite goat, keeps them amused.

Keti likes to shake his head and blow raspberries at them. Sometimes he even head-butts Etabo's bottom.

But the cost of water is rising and Etabo's older siblings have to find work.

Etabo is left to look after the goats alone, with only Keti to keep him company.

Etabo sits in a small acacia tree daydreaming about racing camels. In his dreams he can fly, somersault and even catapult himself onto soft sand dunes.

But his dreams are not enough.

When Etabo goes to see his sister Akiru at work, she lets him pat the horses she looks after.

One nuzzles his hand and licks his face.

"Yuuuuuuckkk!" Etabo screeches.

Although Etabo knows it's against the rules, he begs Akiru to let him ride the horses, but she won't agree.

So instead, Etabo tries to ride...

Chickens…

Cats…

And even Keti…

But none of them will have it.

He prays to Akuj again,
and again Akuj whispers:

"Your dreams are enough."

Akiru watches her brother becoming more and more unhappy and decides to make him a gift.

So she whittles and whittles, and makes Etabo his very own herd of wooden camels.

"Now you can race the wind," Akiru says.

Etabo rushes to the sandy hill with Keti to play
with his wooden camels.

As he races them, he sings to them and they seem
to come to life, right there before his eyes...

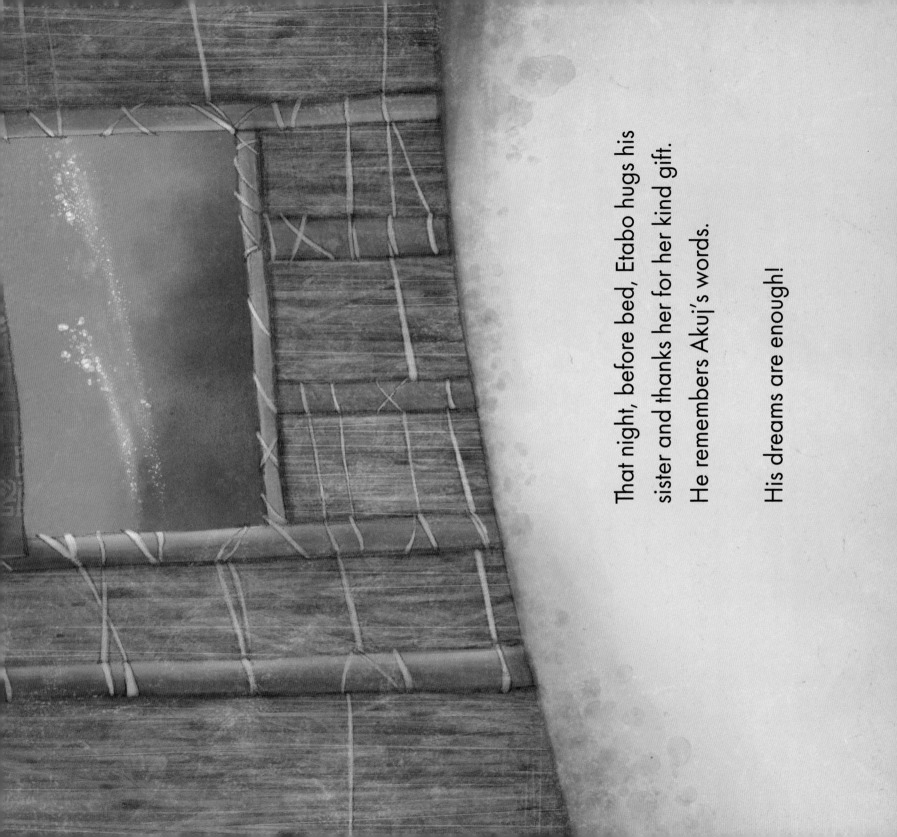

That night, before bed, Etabo hugs his sister and thanks her for her kind gift.

He remembers Akuj's words.

His dreams are enough!

Etabo falls asleep clutching his new best friends.

He drops into a deep dream world where he races
his wooden camels and wins the camel derby.